2

9

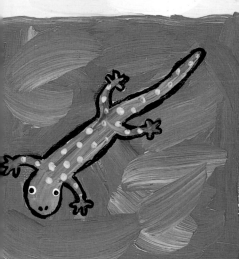

8

6

10

1

For my little baby
safe and snug in my tum
awaiting your arrival
and all the fun to come.

First published in 1999 in Great Britain
by David & Charles Children's Books,
Winchester House, 259-269 Old Marylebone Road, London, NW1 5XJ

2 4 6 8 10 9 7 5 3 1

Illustrations and text © Jane Cabrera 1999.
The right of Jane Cabrera to be identified as the author and illustrator of this work has
been asserted by her in accordancewith the Copyright, Designs and Patents Act 1988.

A CIP catalogue record for this title is available from the British Library.

ISBN 1 86233 137 5

Printed and bound in Belgium

Over in the Meadow

Jane Cabrera

David&Charles
Children's Books

Over in the meadow in the sand in the sun,
Lived Old Mother Turtle and her little turtle **one**.
"Dig," said the mother. "I dig," said the one.
So they dug all day in the sand in the sun.

Over in the meadow where the stream runs blue,
Lived Old Mother Fish and her little fishes two.
"Swim," said the mother. "We swim," said the two.
So they swam all day where the stream runs blue.

Over in the meadow
in a hole in a tree,
lived Old Mother Owl
and her little owls **three**.
"Tu-whoo," said the mother.
"We tu-whoo," said the three.
So they tu-whooed all day
in a hole in a tree.

Over in the meadow by the old barn door,
lived Old Mother Rat and her little ratties **four.**
"Gnaw," said the mother. "We gnaw," said the four.
So they gnawed all day by the old barn door.

Over in the meadow
in a snug beehive,
Lived Old Mother Bee
and her little bees **five.**
"Buzz," said the mother.
"We buzz," said the five.
So they buzzed all day
in a snug beehive.

Over in the meadow in a nest made of sticks,
Lived Old Mother Duck and her little ducks **six.**
"Quack," said the mother, "We quack," said the six.
So they quacked all day in a nest built of sticks.

Over in the meadow where the grass grows even,
Lived Old Mother Frog and her little froggies **seven.**
"Jump," said the mother. "We jump," said the seven.
So they jumped all day where the grass grows even.

Over in the meadow by the old mossy gate,

Lived Old Mother Lizard and her little lizards **eight**.

"Bask," said the mother. "We bask," said the eight.

So they basked all day by the old mossy gate.

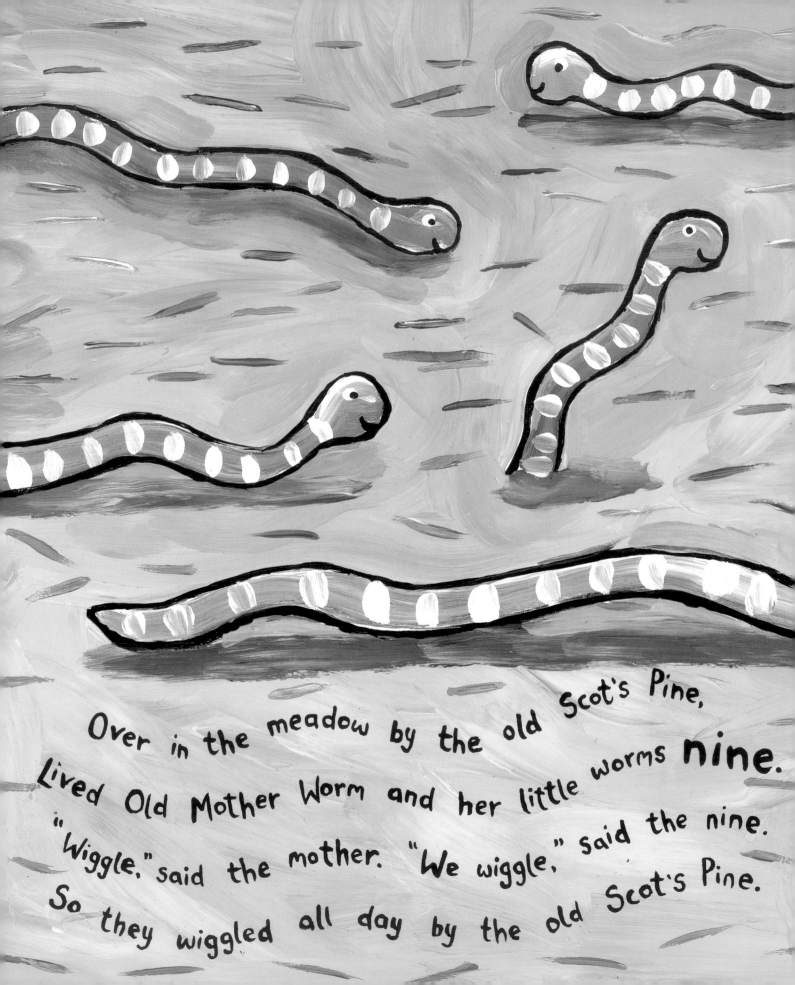

Over in the meadow by the old Scot's Pine,
Lived Old Mother Worm and her little worms **nine.**
"Wiggle," said the mother. "We wiggle," said the nine.
So they wiggled all day by the old Scot's Pine.

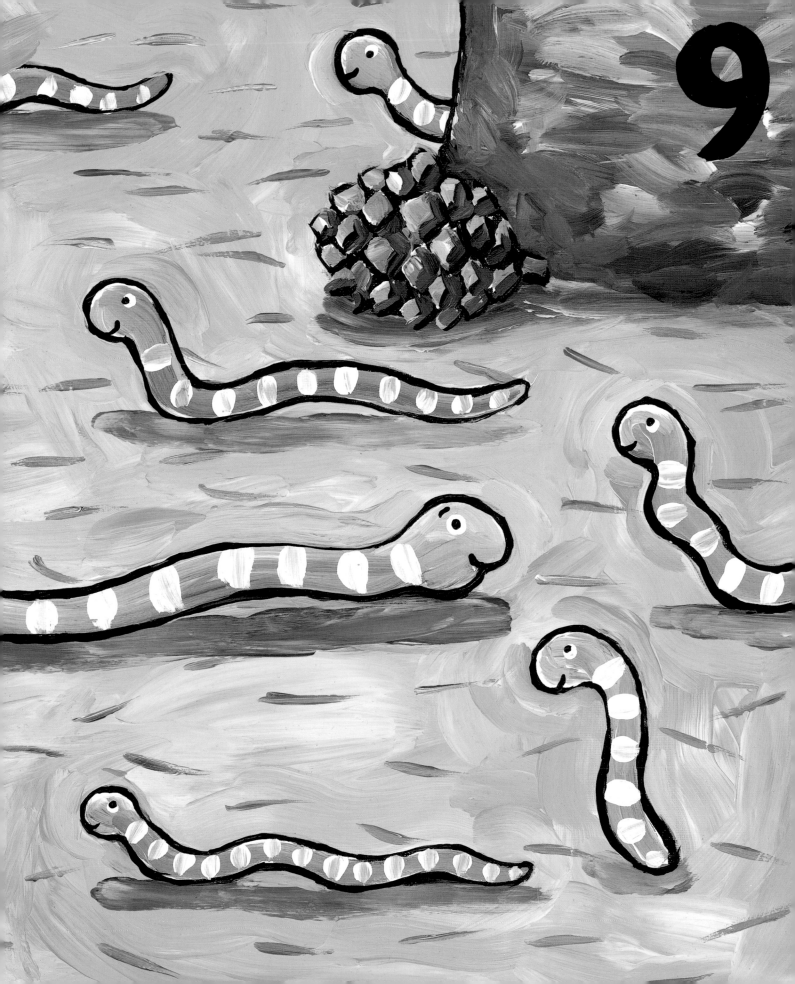

Over in the meadow
in a cosy wee den,
Lived Old Mother Rabbit
and her little rabbits **ten**.
"Twitch," said the mother.
"We twitch," said the ten.
So they twitched all day
in a cosy wee den.

1  **2**

One Turtle | Two Fish

Five Bees | Six Ducks

Nine Worms

Three Owls

Four Rats

Seven Frogs

Eight Lizards

Ten Rabbits